KU-336-269

SOUTHWARK LIBRARIES
SK 2774585 6

A Beowulf Tale

Monster Slayer

A Beowulf Tale
Monster Slayer

Brian Patten

WITH ILLUSTRATIONS BY
Chris Riddell

Barrington Stoke

Published in 2020 in Great Britain by
Barrington Stoke Ltd
18 Walker Street, Edinburgh, EH3 7LP

www.barringtonstoke.co.uk

This story was first published in a different form as
Beowulf and the Monster (Scholastic Ltd, 1999)

This edition based on *Monster Slayer* (Barrington Stoke, 2016)

A CIP catalogue record for this book is available from the British Library upon request

ISBN: 978-1-78112-932-6

Printed in China by Leo

CONTENTS

The Feast to End All Feasts

Long, long ago, when the land was covered in forests, and wolves and demons crouched in every shadow, there lived a powerful king. He was as famous for his kindness as for his strength. When his last great battle was over and there was peace again, he decided to hold a wonderful party to celebrate.

He sent out invitations to the rich and the poor. Then he set about building a gigantic hall where he could hold his special feast.

All his people came to help him build the hall, from the oldest to the youngest, and the new building rose in no time at all in a vast clearing in the forest.

It was a majestic hall, with wooden walls and towers that reached higher than the highest trees. It was the tallest, finest building that had ever been seen in the land. And the King was proud of it. Nothing as grand had existed in his kingdom before. The people called it the Great Hall.

As soon as the Great Hall was finished, the party began. It was to be the feast to end all feasts. It began one morning as the sun rose and then went on day after day, night after night.

Long tables sagged under the weight of the food, and the guests sagged under the effect of the drink. It made their heads spin and made them sing louder and louder and dance more and more wildly.

All this happened in distant times, when wild boars roamed the countryside, and moon-mad wolves slunk past in the night. It was a time when the world was heaped in magic and wonder.

The feast was a roaring success. The music and singing grew louder and louder, and the louder it became the further the sound travelled. At last it was heard beyond the forest, by the one creature no one in their wildest dreams would have invited to the feast.

It was heard by the monster, Grendel.

2

The Monster Grendel

Grendel lived in the fens and the foul-smelling marshland beyond the forest. The marsh was littered with oozing pools and the festering remains of dead otters and decaying fish. No one, not even the bravest warrior, went there. The place reeked of evil.

Evil suited Grendel. He was half man, half monster, a terrible creature stronger almost than any living thing. He was covered in a green, horny skin that no sword could cut, and he came from a race of sea monsters, giants, goblins and other outcasts from the human race.

Grendel was in the habit of sleeping for hundreds of years. When the King's feast began, he had been asleep so long that the King and his subjects had forgotten he ever existed. If they thought of him at all, they remembered him as a creature from legends. That was their big mistake.

And now the sound of music and human laughter had wakened Grendel. He rose from his nest of rats' bones.

He sat among the slithering eels and the smell of decay, and he listened.

Grendel hated music. He hated it because he hated the humans that made it. He hated it with a hatred that burned bright as a star. He hated it as only a demon can hate. It reminded him of what an outcast he was. In his ears that music sounded like the buzzing of flies.

While the King and his warriors feasted and drank, the monster Grendel shook off a hundred years of sleep.

Why should people be happy? he wondered. *Why should they make music and sing and hold great feasts while I sit alone in a stinking bog?* Grendel was full of jealousy and hatred.

I'll destroy their joy, he thought.

Grendel slouched across the marshland and forest towards the Great Hall. As he passed, the creatures of the night shivered with fear and fell silent. The owls stopped hooting. Frogs stopped croaking. The nightingale's song stuck in its throat. Badgers returned to their sets underground. Even the shadows recoiled from Grendel as he flowed through the night like poison spilt from a cup.

Grendel waited, hidden among the trees, until the Great Hall had fallen silent and the last guests had wandered to their homes, sleepy and tired from the feasting.

The King had left his favourite warriors to guard the Great Hall. But there had been peace in the land for so long that they did not take their duty seriously.

They fell asleep, and they did not hear Grendel croaking his terrible song as he moved out from the shadows towards them:

“Sweet human meat’s the best to eat,

And human bones the best to grind.

Human blood will flow again

And terror haunt the human mind.”

A hundred years of sleep had left Grendel hungry. He crashed into the Great Hall and surprised the sleeping warriors. He plucked off their arms and legs as if they were petals. Blood filled the Great Hall. It dripped from the rafters and flowed out into the moonlight. Grendel ate his fill. Then he gathered up the warriors he could not eat into his arms, and the demon slouched back off to his nest in the fetid marshland pools.

Now let them sing, he thought.

The Dreadful Crime

The next morning, people were struck dumb with terror when they saw what had happened in the Great Hall.

It did not take long for them to realise it could have only been Grendel who had committed the dreadful crime. No human could have done what the monster had done, and they saw that the trail of blood led out to the marshland.

The King was in despair. His greatest and most trusted warriors had been killed, and he was too old to wage war against such a creature as Grendel. He sat down on the earth and cried and sang an ancient lament:

"I grow old and my bones grow cold,
The fire of my youth has gone.
My strength is like the ebbing tide
And hopes have I none."

And his people wept with him.

After a hundred years without human blood, the taste was as fresh and sweet as blackberries to Grendel. He came back again and again. Night after night he returned to the village and searched the houses for unwary humans. And each night he sat and brooded in the Great Hall like a bloated spider inside its web.

Soon no one dared to sleep in their homes. People would only visit in the daylight, when they were sure Grendel would not come. And as for the Great Hall, they would not go there day or night.

The Great Hall, their pride and joy, stood empty. Darkness fell upon it. Owls nested in its rafters and rats scurried about its floor.

It was the greatest disaster the King and his people had ever known. At night they all hid in the forest like wild animals. Whenever Grendel found a careless sleeper, he would drag them to the Great Hall and devour them.

4

Warriors from Distant Lands

There was no laughter in the kingdom. No songs. No feasting. No joy.

Stories of the monster's terrible deeds spread far and wide.

Warriors came from distant lands to prove themselves heroes and destroy Grendel, but none was great enough.

The first warrior had a magic bow.

"I'm the greatest warrior of all," he said. "I will destroy Grendel with my bow."

The King hoped against hope that the stranger could fulfil his boast.

At dusk, when Grendel rose up from his nest of rats' bones and came to the village, the warrior took out a magic arrow and aimed it at Grendel's heart. But the arrow might as well have been a feather for all the harm it did.

The next warrior had a magic dagger. It might as well have been a reed for all the harm it did.

Other warriors came, and many lost their lives. Some were fools and others were brave.

All the same, none could defeat Grendel.

He mocked them with his terrible song:

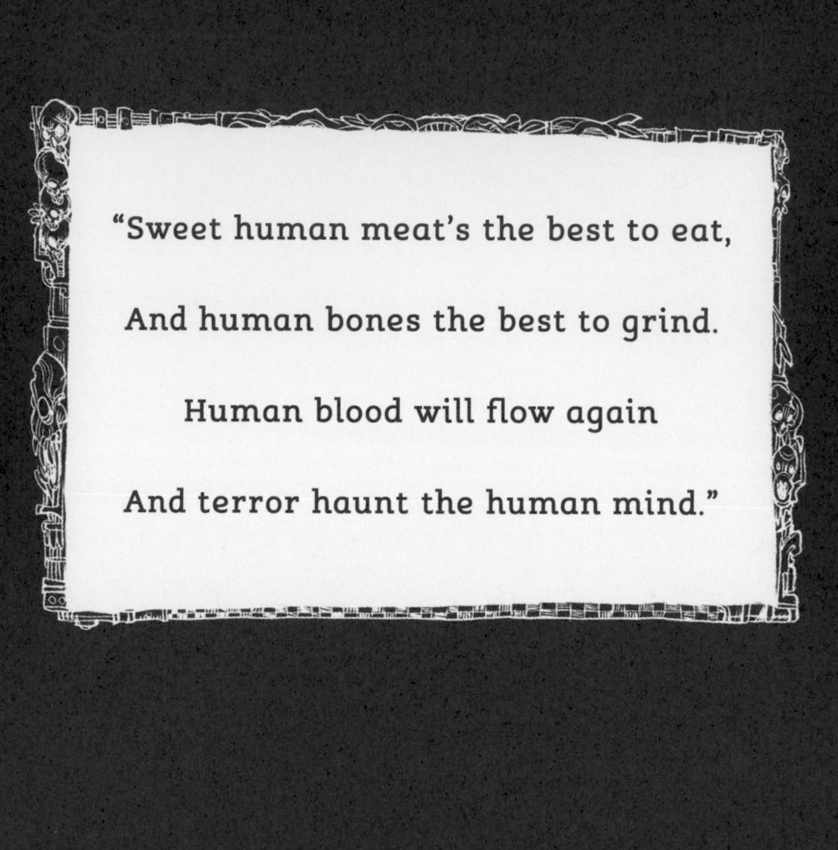

"Sweet human meat's the best to eat,
And human bones the best to grind.
Human blood will flow again
And terror haunt the human mind."

And so the years passed and the dust lay thick as snow in the Great Hall.

People's spirits were broken, and no one took pride in themselves or the land. Crops failed in the fields. Houses fell to rack and ruin. Paths grew over and were forgotten. No warrior would stand against Grendel now. More human bones than rats' bones littered his nest.

Then early one frosty morning, as winter took hold of the kingdom, a boat came sailing over the horizon. It was unlike any other boat that had sailed on the sea before. Its front part was carved with the face of a dragon and its mast looked like the antlers of a stag. The deck glittered with flecks of frost and in the light of the rising sun these were as red as rubies.

It was such a wonderful sight that the people rushed to tell the old King right away. Two of his servants helped him walk to the

cliff top and he stood and watched as the vessel pulled into a rocky bay. A young man stepped from the boat and strode with ease up the cliff's steep path.

The moment the old King looked into the young man's clear eyes he knew who had come to his land. For years, rumours had reached him about a strange young man who lived across the Northern Rim of the world – a boy with the strength of 30 men, but one who was gentle and hard to provoke to anger.

"Are you Beowulf?" he asked.

"Yes," said Beowulf. "And I have come to face Grendel. I would have come some time ago, but the time to face him is written in the stars."

"And do the stars say the time is now?" the King asked.

"Yes," said Beowulf. "Tonight we will light candles in the Great Hall and I will wait for him there."

So many warriors had come before Beowulf and now were nothing more than bones used to line Grendel's nest. The old King felt afraid for Beowulf. But his fear for the young man's life was not as strong as his desire to free his kingdom from the demon who haunted it.

And so he welcomed Beowulf with glad heart, and together they set off for the Great Hall.

When they arrived, the sun had begun to set and the villagers were leaving for their hidey-holes in the forest. The King helped Beowulf light the Great Hall with candles, for Beowulf said the light would confuse Grendel. Then the King departed, troubled in his mind. Beowulf would face the dangers of the night alone.

5

When Shadow Bled into Shadow

Beowulf stood at the door of the Hall as night fell and looked out at the deserted village. The place was as silent as death. Nothing stirred. The light retreated and the shadows thickened. They crept out of the forest and across the marshland like severed fingers and poked Grendel awake.

The monster rose from his nest among the putrid pools, put out his lizard-like tongue and tasted the night. He crooned his vile song:

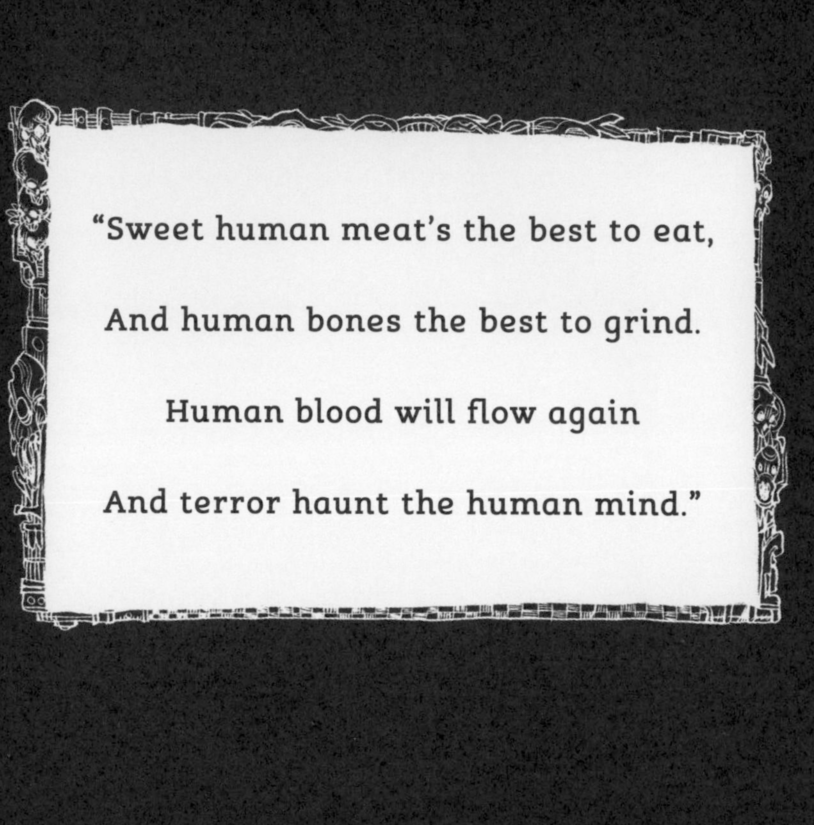

“Sweet human meat’s the best to eat,

And human bones the best to grind.

Human blood will flow again

And terror haunt the human mind.”

When his song was done, Grendel sniffed the air for human blood. Then once again he set off for the Great Hall.

Now Beowulf was the most powerful warrior on earth, stronger than any other man, and he was no fool. He had heard how strong and cunning Grendel could be, and knew he had to be both to match him. He must unsettle Grendel.

He understood that the best fighters kept their wits about them at all times. He must make Grendel so furious and blind with rage that the monster would make a fatal error.

Beowulf took off his sword and put it aside. He knew from the many tales he'd heard that swords were useless on the monster's skin.

When shadow bled into shadow, Grendel came. From the marshy swamps, out of the mists and fogs, the monster made his way to the Great Hall.

He came to the massive door and tried to push it open as he had done night after night, year after year. But the door was locked and bolted. He was furious that the villagers could have done such a thing after so long. He hammered the oak planks with his bare fists and smashed it in, as if it were no more substantial than a wren's nest.

As Grendel entered, his awful shadow filled the Great Hall. His anger grew and grew when he saw that humans had dared to enter before him and fill the place with candles. The Hall's great beams flickered in the light, and cobwebs hung down like freakish decorations. Between the groups of candles were great pools of darkness.

Why had they done this? For what possible reason? For a moment the monster's mind clouded over, and he stood rock-still and puzzled.

This gave time for Beowulf to study his enemy. He stayed hidden among the shadows, but he picked a tiny pebble from the floor and tossed it at Grendel.

Grendel turned, his ears alert to the faintest sound.

“What’s that?” he bellowed.

“A mouse,” Beowulf whispered.

“What mouse is it that smells of human blood and talks with a human tongue?”

"The mouse that will devour you," Beowulf whispered.

In silence, Beowulf climbed up onto the rafters above the Hall, and while Grendel stomped about below, he tossed another pebble.

"What's that?" Grendel roared.

"An owl," Beowulf whispered.

"What owl is it that smells of human blood and talks with a human tongue?"

"The owl that will devour you," said Beowulf.

And then Beowulf dropped from the rafters.

The talk of owls and mice had confused the monster, and he was full of anger that he had been taunted, and so when Beowulf dropped down beside him, he caught him unawares.

Beowulf gripped Grendel's arm and Grendel cried out in surprise. The feel of Beowulf's strong grip was alien to him. Nothing on earth or in the supernatural world had been a threat to him before. He had been the most dangerous thing in the world for hundreds of years.

Now Grendel spun round, flung out his arm and threw Beowulf off balance. But in a moment Beowulf was back. His fist smashed Grendel's jaw and scattered his teeth like black pearls.

As the warrior and the monster rolled on the floor of the Great Hall, first one then the other had the upper hand. Grendel clawed at Beowulf's face till Beowulf was blinded by his own blood. But still he clung to the demon, crushing its neck with the power of 30 men.

In the fury of the fight the Great Hall was destroyed. The great table was smashed to smithereens and splinters stuck in Beowulf and Grendel's flesh. Human and monster blood was sprayed across the scarred walls, and still neither man nor monster gave in.

Then the moment of victory came. There was a sound like the cracking of a branch and the bone in Grendel's right arm snapped. For the first and only time, he tasted defeat.

He bellowed with despair and wiped the blood from his eyes to look for the door, and escape. But Beowulf held his good arm in a grip no man on earth could break or stand,

and the monster howled in agony as he struggled to free himself.

At last, with a final cry, Grendel managed to drag himself free. He staggered out of the Hall, leaving behind him a river of blood. In his fury to escape, his arm had been torn off and left in Beowulf's iron-like grip. Beowulf looked at it in horror and flung it away.

Back across the marshy swamp the monster stumbled, into the mists and fogs. Soon he was home, and as the last flickerings of life faded from him, he sank down into the lake by the foul marsh. Down he sank, deeper and deeper into the stinking depths, dying as he reached the very place of his birth.

And in that secret place, an even greater monster waited.

6

The Hag

The next morning the sun rose over a different world. It glittered on beads of water where the frost had melted, and the Great Hall's roof shone as if it were made of silver.

The old King wept with joy when he heard how the fight had ended.

He hugged Beowulf like a son and ordered his men to clean out and repair the Great Hall. They nailed Grendel's arm above the door so

everyone could see for themselves how great Beowulf's victory had been.

As the news spread, so Beowulf's fame spread. He was showered with gift after gift in thanks – a sword with a golden handle, a helmet embedded with jewels, seven of the finest stallions in the land.

The villagers came out of their hidey-holes in the forest. Now there was food and music again. People drank themselves dizzy. They wore themselves out dancing. Then, after the feast, they returned to their homes for the first time in years.

Beowulf slept in the best room in the King's house. He fell into a deep sleep, tired from his great victory.

But then something new stirred out in the fens and marshlands. Again, evil was abroad. Pools bubbled with poison and the Hag appeared. The first and most terrible witch in the world.

It was Grendel's mother, rising to seek her revenge on those who had slain her son.

The Hag came that night. She loped along the paths in the marsh like a hungry wolf. She was bent double with age, yet she was still almost twice the size of a human being. She swept into the village, blind with grief and rage.

"Who killed my son?" she howled. "What man killed him?"

But her fury was so great that no one could speak. She dragged them from their beds, sank her teeth into their necks and silenced them for ever. And then she was gone again, with a trail of death and destruction behind her.

When an old man who had escaped the Hag described her to the King, the King remembered the legend of how Grendel's mother lived deep below the lake in the marsh, and he knew it was she who had caused such mayhem.

The King called for Beowulf and begged him to try and destroy her, as he had destroyed her son.

The King told Beowulf of how, in the legend, the Hag's lair was protected by three chambers, and each of the chambers was blocked by three gigantic stones. The stones were so heavy no human could lift them.

"Then we are lost," Beowulf said. "She is well protected."

"Perhaps not," the King said. "The legend also says a clever man can make the stones move of their own accord."

"How can stones move of their own accord?" Beowulf asked.

The King shrugged. "How did you kill a monster? There are many things in the world we cannot explain, Beowulf. You must try for all our sakes," he said.

And so Beowulf left the King and his people to care for the wounded, and he set off alone to find Grendel's mother. She had left the village so covered in blood that her tracks were easy to follow. The blood-splattered trail led him along the marshland paths. It led past groves of twisted trees and broken stumps grey with moss.

Rats scurried along the path ahead of him. Crows blinked their tiny red eyes and hopped from tangled branch to tangled branch like little spies.

It was still daylight, but the closer Beowulf came to the Hag's lair, the colder the day seemed. He was sure she knew he was coming.

The path snaked deep into the deadly marshes. It passed stinking pools and crossed over weed-choked streams where toads croaked and sang like a choir of witches. Beowulf came to the edge of a dark lake where a yellow mist shut out the sun. The whole of the place felt lifeless. The air itself seemed stale and sour, trapped under a canopy of gloomy clouds.

Near the middle of the lake he saw Grendel's nest, abandoned now.

Beowulf's heart drummed fast as he prepared to face the Hag.

He clipped on his vest of chainmail. In his belt he hung a sword hardened by the blood of battles. He polished his dagger with poison.

With slow, deep breaths, he waded into the lake.

Beowulf gripped his sword as he sank down into the murky depths. Eels wrapped themselves around his legs. Leeches clung to his cheeks. He ignored them and he sank deeper and deeper until he came to a thin crust of rock on the lake's bottom. He thrust his sword into it as easily as a child might thrust a spoon into a pie.

The river-bed opened, and Beowulf fell into the underground chambers that led to the Hag's lair.

7

The Riddle Stones

It was here in the Hag's lair that Beowulf came upon the body of Grendel.

It had been laid out with love on a stone slab, and Beowulf felt a stab of confusion as he looked upon that awful face. To the Hag perhaps it was a lovely face, the face of her only son.

But Beowulf could not afford to feel sorry for her. How many other people could she kill?

And what other monsters would she send to the face of the earth if he let her live? It was his purpose to slay her.

Beowulf found the first of the three huge stones that blocked the way to the Hag's lair. It was so huge he did not even attempt to move it. Instead he studied the stone and remembered what the old King had told him.

"How can a clever man make a stone move of its own accord?" Beowulf wondered out loud.

As soon as he spoke, the stone began to change. Where its centre had been smooth, now two thin lines appeared. They grew wider, and as Beowulf gazed, a pair of lips grew upon the surface of the stone.

"I am the first of the Riddle Stones," it said. "Answer my riddle and I will move aside." There was a moment's silence, and then the stone spoke again:

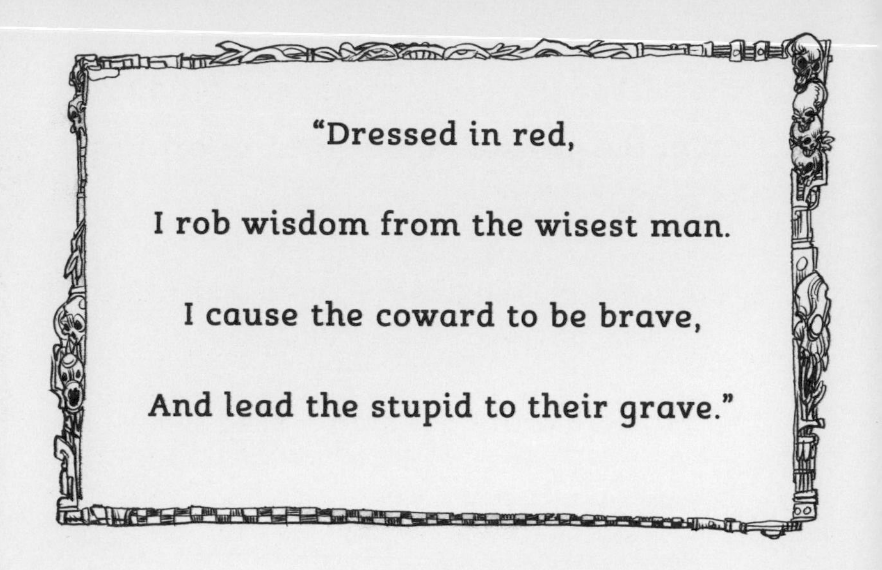

"Dressed in red,

I rob wisdom from the wisest man.

I cause the coward to be brave,

And lead the stupid to their grave."

Beowulf thought the riddle was easy.

"Wine is the answer," he said. "Even the wisest men are fools when they are drunk."

He was right and the stone moved aside. Behind it was a second chamber. Here an even greater Riddle Stone stood in his path, and the same thing happened. Lips grew out of the stone and it spoke to him.

"I am the second of the Riddle Stones," it said. "Answer my riddle and I too will move aside."

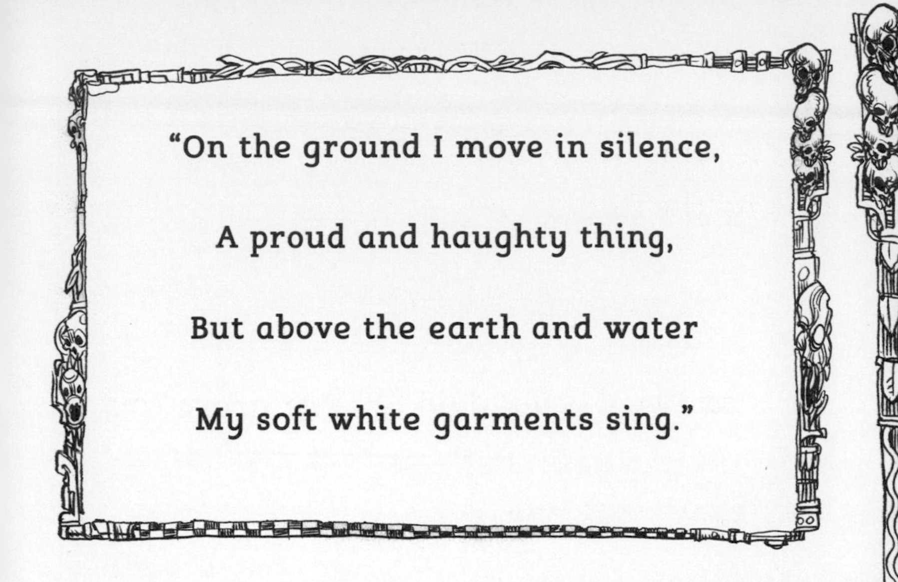

"On the ground I move in silence,

A proud and haughty thing,

But above the earth and water

My soft white garments sing."

Beowulf found this riddle harder than the first, but again he found the answer. "It is Swan," he said. "A swan does not speak but when it flies through the air its wings make a sound like singing."

The second of the Riddle Stones moved aside.

In the third and final chamber he found the most massive stone of all.

Beowulf did not know it, but in the world above him night had fallen. The darker it grew, the more powerful the Hag became. She was moving about now, vast and wolf-like beyond the final stone.

It, too, spoke to Beowulf.

“I am the third Riddle Stone. Answer my riddle and you will find the Hag who haunts the human mind.”

Beowulf listened as the lips in the stone sneered at him.

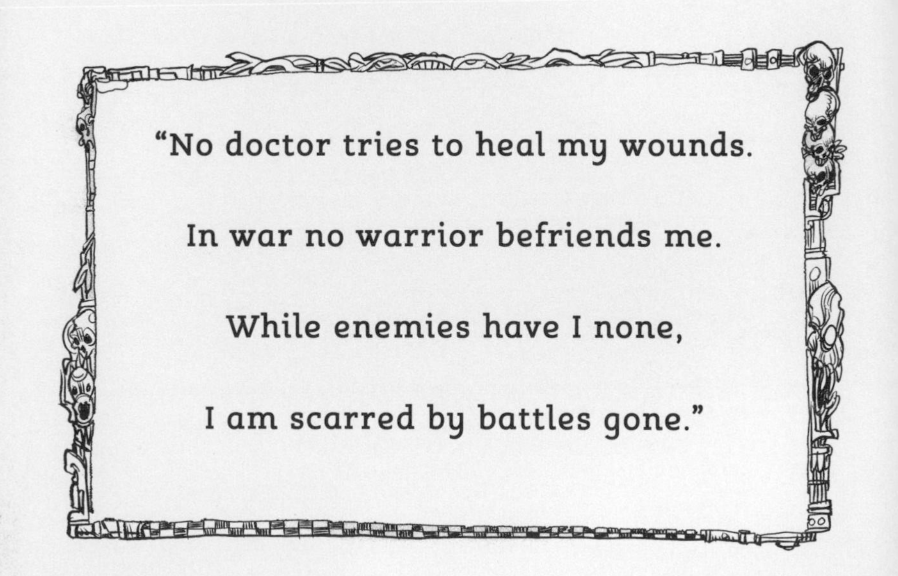

“No doctor tries to heal my wounds.

In war no warrior befriends me.

While enemies have I none,

I am scarred by battles gone.”

Because he was a warrior, Beowulf found this riddle the simplest of all. “In war no warrior befriends a shield,” he said, “so Shield is the answer.”

Again he was right, and the final stone rolled aside.

A Nest of Bones

Beyond the stone, Grendel's mother sat crouched in a nest of bones. From her eyes shone a green light that lit up the chamber's walls and made Beowulf's shadow dance upon them like a doll.

Like Grendel, she too was covered in scales. The small, stiff hairs on her back were alive with lice. She swayed to and fro, now mewing like a cat, now growling like a wolf, and never for a moment did she take her eyes from Beowulf's face.

She leaped towards him, and as she did so, Beowulf swung his massive sword. The end was more swift than he could have ever imagined.

The sword struck the side of her neck with crushing force and shattered like glass. He flung the broken weapon aside. As she leaped upon him again, he grabbed a human bone from her nest and thrust it into her throat with almost super-human force. A fountain of green blood burst from her mouth and the Hag fell back, dead.

Only when her body had turned cold did Beowulf approach it. He had overcome her with such ease that he hardly dared believe his good fortune. He waited until even the lice had deserted the body, then he dragged the Hag and her son to the lake's surface, and he swam with them to the shore.

The bodies were laid out in the Great Hall, plain for all to see. This time, no one could doubt that the kingdom had been made safe by Beowulf.

Again the old King wept with happiness. Again fabulous gifts were showered on Beowulf. Again a great feast was held in his honour. Again many stories were told of his victory over the monsters.

This is but one of them.

Our books are tested
for children and young people by
children and young people.

Thanks to everyone who consulted on
a manuscript for their time and effort in
helping us to make our books better
for our readers.